"*THE YOUNG VISITERS* is the greatest novel ever written by a nine-year-old," writes Walter Kendrick in his new introduction to this delightful book for adults, out of print on this side of the Atlantic for over thirty-five years. American readers are in for a treat.

The English nine-year-old was Daisy Ashford who, in 1890, wrote this merry tale of unrequited love, romance, and social ambition in pencil, in a twopenny notebook, at her family's comfortable home near Brighton. In the English edition's original preface, J.M. Barrie predicted, "[it will give pause to any who dare to spend a] weekend in a house where there may be a novelist of nine years."

"There is evidence that she thoroughly enjoyed the run of her parents' library, and, unseen and unheard, revelled in the conversation of her elders."

— *Athenaeum*

"The quaintly pretentious style and the engaging worldly wisdom of the little author make it luscious reading."

— *Dial*

# THE YOUNG VISITERS

## DAISY ASHFORD

THE AUTHOR

# THE
# YOUNG VISITERS

OR, MR SALTEENA'S PLAN

BY
**DAISY ASHFORD**

WITH A PREFACE BY
Walter Kendrick

ACADEMY CHICAGO PUBLISHERS

Published in 1991 and
Reprinted in 2000 by
Academy Chicago Publishers
363 West Erie Street
Chicago, Illinois 60610

Published by arrangement with Chatto & Windus, Ltd.

Printed and bound in the U.S.A.

**Library of Congress Cataloging-in-Publication Data**

Ashford, Daisy
   The young visiters, or, Mr. Salteena's plan / by Daisy Ashford ;
   with a preface by Walter Kendrick.
      p.   cm.
      ISBN 0-89733-365-9
      1. Children's writings, English.  I. Title.  II. Title: Young
   visiters.  III. Title: Mr. Salteena's plan.
   PR6001.S44Y7    1991
823'.912—dc20                          91-32445
                                              CIP

# CONTENTS

# PREFACE

*THE Young Visiters* is the greatest novel ever written by a nine-year-old. Daisy Ashford wrote it, around 1890, in her family's comfortable home at Lewes, near Brighton, England. The manuscript gathered dust in a drawer until 1919, when someone—history is vaguer than Ashford's fiction—brought it to light. The unknown but perceptive rescuer sent Ashford's twopenny notebook, crammed with her large, clear handwriting, to Chatto and Windus, who have kept *The Young Visiters* in print ever since in Britain where Ashford's stature has grown with time. In 1985 she won the distinction of an entry in Margaret Drabble's fifth edition of *The Oxford Companion to English Literature.*

Ashford's American fortunes have been spottier. Though the long-defunct firm of George H. Doran published *The Young Visiters* here in 1919—and enjoyed enough success to follow it up in 1920 with a collection of minor works, *Daisy Ashford: Her Book,* — Ashford failed to become a standard author on this side of the Atlantic. *Her Book* was not reprinted; *The Young Visiters* wobbled in and out of print until the mid-50s, when it, too, dropped into oblivion, at least as far as publishers were concerned. This Academy Chicago edition marks the first American appearance of *The Young Visiters* in some 35 years.

American readers never wholly forgot Ashford's novel. It remained popular in secondhand bookstores, where even a battered copy was sure to sell within hours of showing up on the shelf. But America pigeonholed *The Young Visiters* as a children's book, and an arcane one at that, suitable for rather studious preteens (mainly girls) or those with Anglophile parents. This was a gross injustice. Children can get great pleasure from *The Young Visiters*— as they can from *War and Peace* — but Ashford did not have nine-year-olds in mind while she wrote. What she had in mind was the truth of human experience, as she had seen it and read about it in novels written for adults.

I would lay the blame for juvenilizing *The Young Visiters* on Sir James M. Barrie, creator of Peter Pan, who wrote a treacly preface to the 1919 edition. Barrie drew a precious picture of little Daisy at work, now "with the tongue firmly clenched between her teeth," now with "her head to the side and and her tongue well out." He imagined her sucking her thumb and called her the "blazing child." The British stomach such goop better than Americans do; they seem to place a smaller premium on growing up. Barrie, however, falsified *The Young Visiters* for all readers when he made it out to be merely the product of a precocious imagination. It is that, of course, but it is also a Victorian novel in miniature, a tidy précis of English fiction circa 1890.

*The Young Visiters* has two themes: love and social advancement. So does *Pride and Prejudice*. It has a double plot, the specialty of Dickens, George Eliot, Trollope, and the other great mid-Victorians. Ashford's spelling and punctuation are hilariously idiosyncratic; she gets swoony about "champaigne" and "sumpshous" furnishings. But she knows what such hard words mean, even when she falls back on phonetics. And her viewpoint throughout is strictly unsentimental. You may laugh with joy, but you dare not patronize her.

Ethel Monticue and Bernard Clark provide the love plot, which climaxes by the Thames near Windsor Castle:

Bernard placed one arm tightly round her. When will you marry me Ethel he uttered you must be my wife it has come to that I love you so intensly that if you say no I shall perforce dash my body to the brink of yon muddy river he panted wildly.

Oh dont do that implored Ethel breathing rather hard.

She swoons, but as they board their boat, sobriety returns:

I trust you have not got any illness my darling murmered Bernard as he helped her in.

Oh no I am very strong said Ethel I fainted from joy she added to explain matters.

Oh I see said Bernard handing her a cushon well some people do he added kindly...

No doubt Ashford had read her share of romances. But she also possessed sturdy British common sense that reined the romance in.

Levelheadedness also prevails in the companion plot, the story of Alfred Salteena. His "Plan," announced in the

novel's subtitle, is to get himself trans-
formed into the most ineffable of English achievements, a gentleman. At first
Mr. Salteena's plight seems hopeless: "I
am not quite a gentleman," he admits,
"but you would hardly notice it but cant
be helped anyhow." Bernard, however,
writes him a letter of introduction to the
Earl of Clincham, who lives in the "Crystal Pallace." The Earl "might rub you
up," advises Bernard, "and by mixing with
him you would probably grow more
seemly." Mr Salteena sets off at once for
London, leaving Bernard and Ethel to fall
rather conventionally in love. But there
is nothing conventional about Ashford's
Crystal Palace. It is the grand set piece of
*The Young Visiters* and a triumph of imagination.

The real Crystal Palace couldn't hold a
candle to it. Constructed in Hyde Park to
house the Great Exhibition of 1851, the
vast glass-and-iron structure made a bril-
liant showplace for the products of British industry and exotic plunder from the
reaches of the Empire. Some six million
people came to gape at it during its years
of operation. In 1852, the Crystal Palace
was dismantled and reassembled south
of the Thames, in Sydenham, where it
became the center of an amusement park.

It was still functioning when Ashford wrote *The Young Visiters* — it lasted 'till 1936, when it was destroyed by fire — and she may well have visited there. Her Crystal Palace features "a lovely fountain in the middle," just like the real one, as well as "little stalls where you could buy sweets and lemonade." But Ashford's version also contains "the Privite Compartments," in which the entire British aristocracy appears to dwell.

The Compartments resemble an expensive residential hotel, complete with central heating. Each nobleman's name is affixed to his door; Mr Salteena gains admission to the Earl of Clincham's rooms merely by ringing the bell. The earl greets him airily, like a true aristocrat, but turns blunt on the question of finances: "You see these compartments are the haunts of the Aristockracy said the earl and they are kept going by peaple who have got something funny in their family and who want to be less mere if you comprehend." Mr. Salteena does. He forks over £10 ( in gold), which the earl pockets. "It will be £42 before I have done with you," says the complaisant blueblood, "but you can pay me here and there as convenient."

Thus Ashford accounts, with considerable acuity, for an institution whose survival continues to puzzle sager heads than hers. Perhaps she, too, had wondered what earthly purpose was served by earls; perhaps she had overheard her well-off but untitled elders gossiping breathlessly about their betters. Wherever she found her materials, her imagination fused them into a fantasy that comes scarily close to truth. More than one social critic has grimly observed that the chief use of Britain's aristocracy is to make the middle class "less mere." A century ago, nine-year-old Ashford figured that out on her own.

The system works, however, at least for Mr. Salteena. At the Crystal Palace, he undergoes a crash course in costume and manners, culminating in a jaunt to Buckingham Palace, where he meets the chatty Prince of Wales ("all I want is peace and quiut and a little fun," confides the future Edward VII). In a flash, Mr Salteena has aquired "a smart suit of green velvit with knickerbockers compleat" and " any day might be seen in Hyde park or Pickadilly galloping madly after the Royal Carrage." No piffle about blood or breeding: for Ashford, clothes make the gentleman— or the prince.

Though Mr. Salteena looks "bitterly sad" at Ethel and Bernard's wedding—he has nursed a secret passion for her from the start — he consoles himself with Bessie Topp, "a plesant girl of 18 with a round red face and rather stary eyes." The Salteenas have 10 children ("five of each"), but as the years pass, Mr. Salteena grows "very morose." He cannot forget Ethel, and eventually he seeks solace in religion. The earl's marriage also sours. Only Bernard and Ethel stay in love " to the bitter end"—"and they had a nice house too." Romances may have shown Ashford any number of happy endings, but her own down-to-earth sense of reality led her to wind up *The Young Visiters* on a distinctly mixed and muted note.

Ashford did not slack off after the hidden triumph of *The Young Visiters*. She moved on to her most ambitious work, "The Hangman's Daughter" (published in *Her Book*), completed when she was 14. It is more than twice the length of *The Young Visiters* and remained Ashford's personal favorite, for the rather ominous reason that "I put so much more effort into it." The effort shows. "The Hangman's Daughter" has its moments, but on the whole it's a labored performance; evidently, Ashford's rare talent was already in decline. Once she left school, she recalled decades later, she gave up all ambition "to become an authoress." She lived in apparently contented obscurity till 1972, when she died at the age of 91.

"Only once in an eon or so," archly remarked Irvin S. Cobb in 1920, "is it vouchsafed a writer to write a masterpiece at the age of nine years." Ashford's eon continues. But archness like Cobb's, and cutesiness like Barrie's, eventually threw a pall over the book that has deprived American readers of a rare and enduring delight. Ashford's masterpiece truly deserves the overworked adjective "unique": there is nothing else like it, and nothing can match the special pleasure it gives.

—WALTER KENDRICK
NEW YORK
JULY, 1991

# THE
# YOUNG VISITERS

## CHAPTER 1

### QUITE A YOUNG GIRL

MR SALTEENA was an elderly man of 42 and
was fond of asking peaple to stay with him.
He had quite a young girl staying with him
of 17 named Ethel Monticue. Mr Salteena
had dark short hair and mustache and
wiskers which were very black and twisty.
He was middle sized and he had very pale
blue eyes. He had a pale brown suit but
on Sundays he had a black one and he had a
topper every day as he thorght it more be-
coming. Ethel Monticue had fair hair done
on the top and blue eyes. She had a blue
velvit frock which had grown rarther short
in the sleeves. She had a black straw hat
and kid gloves.

One morning Mr Salteena came down to brekfast and found Ethel had come down first which was strange. Is the tea made Ethel he said rubbing his hands. Yes said Ethel and such a quear shaped parcel has come for you  Yes indeed it was a quear shape parcel it was a hat box tied down very tight and a letter stuffed between the string. Well well said Mr Salteena parcels do turn quear I will read the letter first and so saying he tore open the letter and this is what it said

MY DEAR ALFRED.

I want you to come for a stop with me so I have sent you a top hat wraped up in tishu paper inside the box. Will you wear it staying with me because it is very uncommon. Please bring one of your young ladies whichever is the prettiest in the face.

I remain Yours truely

BERNARD CLARK.

Well said Mr Salteena I shall take you to stay Ethel and fancy him sending me a top hat. Then Mr S. opened the box and there lay the most splendid top hat of a lovly rich tone rarther like grapes with a ribbon round compleat.

Well said Mr Salteena peevishly I dont know if I shall like it the bow of the ribbon is too flighty for my age. Then he sat down and eat the egg which Ethel had so kindly laid for him. After he had finished his meal he got down and began to write to Bernard Clark he ran up stairs on his fat legs and took out his blotter with a loud sniff and this is what he wrote

MY DEAR BERNARD

Certinly I shall come and stay with you next Monday I will bring Ethel Monticue commonly called Miss M. She is very active and pretty. I do hope I shall enjoy myself with you. I am fond of digging in the garden and I am parshial to ladies if they are nice I suppose it is my nature. I am not quite a gentleman but you would hardly notice it but cant be helped anyhow. We will come by the 3-15.

> Your old and valud friend
> ALFRED SALTEENA.

Perhaps my readers will be wondering why Bernard Clark had asked Mr Salteena to stay with him. He was a lonely man in a remote spot and he liked peaple and partys but he did not know many. What rot muttered Bernard Clark as he read Mr Salteenas letter. He was rarther a presumshious man.

The Young Visiters
or Mr Salteena's plan

by Daisy Ashford

Chap 1
Quite a young girl

Mr Salteena was an elderly man of 42 and was fond of asking people to stay with him. He had quite a young girl staying with him of 17 named Ethel Monticue. Mr Salteena had dark short hair and mustache and whiskers which were very black and twisty. He was middle sized and he

THE FIRST PAGE OF THE ORIGINAL MANUSCRIPT

# CHAPTER 2

## STARTING GAILY

WHEN the great morning came Mr Salteena did not have an egg for his brekfast in case he should be sick on the jorney.

What top hat will you wear asked Ethel.

I shall wear my best black and my white alpacka coat to keep off the dust and flies replied Mr Salteena.

I shall put some red ruge on my face said Ethel because I am very pale owing to the drains in this house.

You will look very silly said Mr Salteena with a dry laugh.

Well so will you said Ethel in a snappy tone and she ran out of the room with a very superier run throwing out her legs behind and her arms swinging in rithum.

[25]

Well said the owner of the house she has a most idiotick run.

Presently Ethel came back in her best hat and a lovly velvit coat of royal blue. Do I look nice in my get up she asked.

Mr Salteena survayed her. You look rarther rash my dear your colors dont quite match your face but never mind I am just going up to say goodbye to Rosalind the housemaid.

Well dont be long said Ethel. Mr S. skipped upstairs to Rosalinds room. Goodbye Rosalind he said I shall be back soon and I hope I shall enjoy myself.

I make no doubt of that sir said Rosalind with a blush as Mr Salteena silently put 2/6 on the dirty toilet cover.

Take care of your bronkitis said Mr S. rarther bashfully and he hastilly left the room waving his hand carelessly to the housemaid.

Come along cried Ethel powdering her nose in the hall let us get into the cab. Mr

Salteena did not care for powder but he was an unselfish man so he dashed into the cab. Sit down said Ethel as the cabman waved his whip you are standing on my luggage. Well I am paying for the cab said Mr S. so I might be allowed to put my feet were I like.

They traveled 2nd class in the train and Ethel was longing to go first but thought perhaps least said soonest mended. Mr Salteena got very excited in the train about his visit. Ethel was calm but she felt excited inside. Bernard has a big house said Mr. S. gazing at Ethel he is inclined to be rich.

Oh indeed said Ethel looking at some cows flashing past the window. Mr. S. felt rarther disheartened so he read the paper till the train stopped and the porters shouted Rickamere station. We had better collect our traps said Mr Salteena and just then a very exalted footman in a cocked hat and olive green uniform put his head in

[27]

at the window. Are you for Rickamere Hall he said in impressive tones.

Well yes I am said Mr Salteena and so is this lady.

Very good sir said the noble footman if you will alight I will see to your luggage there is a convayance awaiting you.

Oh thankyou thankyou said Mr. S. and he and Ethel stepped along the platform. Outside they found a lovely cariage lined with olive green cushons to match the footman and the horses had green bridles and bows on their manes and tails. They got gingerly in. Will he bring our luggage asked Ethel nervously.

I expect so said Mr Salteena lighting a very long cigar.

Do we tip him asked Ethel quietly.

Well no I dont think so not yet we had better just thank him perlitely.

Just then the footman staggered out with the bagage. Ethel bowed gracefully over the door of the cariage and Mr S. waved his hand as each bit of luggage was hoisted up to make sure it was all there. Then he said thankyou my good fellow very politely. Not at all sir said the footman and touching his cocked hat he jumped actively to the box.

I was right not to tip him whispered Mr Salteena the thing to do is to leave 2/6 on your dressing table when your stay is over.

Does he find it asked Ethel who did not really know at all how to go on at a visit. I beleeve so replied Mr Salteena anyhow it is quite the custom and we cant help it if he does not. Now my dear what do you think of the sceenery

Very nice said Ethel gazing at the rich fur rug on her knees. Just then the cariage rolled into a beautifull drive with tall trees and big red flowers growing amid shiny dark leaves. Presently the haughty coachman pulled up with a great clatter at a huge front door with tall pillers each side a big iron bell and two very clean scrapers. The doors flung open as if by majic causing

[29]

Ethel to jump and a portly butler appeared on the scene with a very shiny shirt front and a huge pale face. Welcome sir he exclaimed good naturedly as Mr Salteena alighted rarther quickly from the viacle and please to step inside.

Mr Salteena stepped in as bid followed by Ethel. The footman again struggled with the luggage and the butler Francis Minnit by name kindly lent a hand. The hall was very big and hung round with guns and mats and ancesters giving it a gloomy but a grand air. The butler then showed them down a winding corridoor till he came to a door which he flung open shouting Mr Salteena and a lady sir.

A tall man of 29 rose from the sofa. He was rarther bent in the middle with very nice long legs fairish hair and blue eyes. Hullo Alf old boy he cried so you have got here all safe and no limbs broken.

None thankyou Bernard replied Mr Salteena shaking hands and let me introduce

Miss Monticue she is very pleased to come for this visit. Oh yes gasped Ethel blushing through her red ruge. Bernard looked at her keenly and turned a dark red. I am glad to see you he said I hope you will enjoy it but I have not arranged any partys yet as I dont know anybody.

Dont worry murmered Ethel I dont mix much in Socierty and she gave him a dainty smile.

I expect you would like some tea said Bernard I will ring.

Yes indeed we should said Mr Salteena egerly. Bernard pealed on the bell and the butler came in with a stately walk.

Tea please Minnit crid Bernard Clark. With pleshure sir replied Minnit with a deep bow. A glorious tea then came in on a gold tray two kinds of bread and butter a lovly jam role and lots of sugar cakes. Ethels eyes began to sparkle and she made several remarks during the meal. I expect

you would now like to unpack said Bernard
when it was over.

Well yes that is rarther an idear said Mr
Salteena.

I have given the best spare room to Miss
Monticue said Bernard with a gallant bow
and yours turning to Mr Salteena opens out
of it so you will be nice and friendly both
the rooms have big windows and a handsome view.

How charming said Ethel. Yes well let
us go up replied Bernard and he led the
way up many a winding stairway till they
came to an oak door with some lovly swans
and bull rushes painted on it. Here we
are he cried gaily. Ethels room was indeed
a handsome compartment with purple silk
curtains and a 4 post bed draped with the
same shade. The toilit set was white and
mouve and there were some violets in a
costly varse. Oh I say cried Ethel in supprise. I am glad you like it said Bernard
and here we have yours Alf. He opened

the dividing doors and portrayed a smaller but dainty room all in pale yellow and wild primroses. My own room is next the bath room said Bernard it is decerated dark red as I have somber tastes. The bath room has got a tip up bason and a hose thing for washing your head.

A good notion said Mr Salteena who was secretly getting jellus.

Here we will leave our friends to unpack and end this Chapter.

## CHAPTER 3

WHEN they had unpacked Mr Salteena and
Ethel went downstairs to dinner. Mr Salteena had put on a compleat evening suit
as he thought it was the correct idear and
some ruby studs he had got at a sale.
Ethel had on a dress of yellaw silk covered
with tulle which was quite in the fashion
and she had on a necklace which Mr Salteena gave her for a birthday present. She
looked very becomeing and pretty and Bernard heaved a sigh as he gave her his arm
to go into dinner. The butler Minnit was
quite ready for the fray standing up very
stiff and surrounded by two footmen in
green plush and curly white wigs who were
called Charles and Horace.

Well said Mr Salteena lapping up his

[34]

turtle soup you have a very sumpshous house Bernard.

His friend gave a weary smile and swollowed a few drops of sherry wine. It is fairly decent he replied with a bashful glance at Ethel after our repast I will show you over the premisis.

Many thanks said Mr Salteena getting rarther flustered with his forks.

You ourght to give a ball remarked Ethel you have such large compartments.

Yes there is room enough sighed Bernard we might try a few steps and meanwhile I might get to know a few peaple.

So you might responded Ethel giving him a speaking look.

Mr Salteena was growing a little peevish but he cheered up when the Port wine came on the table and the butler put round some costly finger bowls. He did not have any in his own house and he followed Bernard Clarks advice as to what to do with them. After dinner Ethel played some

[35]

merry tunes on the piano and Bernard responded with a rarther loud song in a base voice and Ethel clapped him a good deal. Then Mr Salteena asked a few riddles as he was not musicle. Then Bernard said shall I show you over my domain and they strolled into the gloomy hall.

I see you have a lot of ancesters said Mr Salteena in a jelous tone, who are they.

Well said Bernard they are all quite correct. This is my aunt Caroline she was rarther exentrick and quite old.

So I see said Mr Salteena and he passed on to a lady with a very tight waist and quearly shaped. That is Mary Ann Fudge my grandmother I think said Bernard she was very well known in her day.

Why asked Ethel who was rarther curious by nature.

Well I dont quite know said Bernard but she was and he moved away to the next picture. It was of a man with a fat smiley face and a red ribbon round him and a lot of medals. My great uncle Ambrose Fudge said Bernard carelessly.

He looks a thourough ancester said Ethel kindly.

Well he was said Bernard in a proud tone he was really the Sinister son of Queen Victoria.

Not really cried Ethel in excited tones but what does that mean.

Well I dont quite know said Bernard Clark it puzzles me very much but ancesters do turn quear at times.

Peraps it means god son said Mr Salteena in an inteligent voice.

Well I dont think so said Bernard but I mean to find out.

It is very grand anyhow said Ethel.

It is that replied her host geniully.

Who is this said Mr Salteena halting at a picture of a lady holding up some grapes and smiling a good deal.

Her name was called Minnie Pilato responded Bernard she was rarther far back

[37]

but a real relation and she was engaged to the earl of Tullyvarden only it did not quite come off.

What a pity crid Ethel.

Yes it was rarther replied Bernard but she marrid a Captain in the Navy and had seven children so she was quite alright.

Here Mr Salteena thourght he had better go to bed as he had had a long jornney. Bernard always had a few prayers in the hall and some whiskey afterwards as he was rarther pious but Mr Salteena was not very adicted to prayers so he marched up to bed. Ethel stayed as she thourght it would be a good thing. The butler came in as he was a very holy man and Bernard piously said the Our Father and a very good hymm called I will keep my anger down and a Decad of the Rosary. Ethel chimed in quiutly and Francis Minnit was most devout and Ethel thourght what a good holy family she was stopping with. So I will end my chapter.

# CHAPTER 4

## MR SALTEENAS PLAN

MR SALTEENA woke up rarther early next day and was supprised and delighted to find Horace the footman entering with a cup of tea.

Oh thankyou my man said Mr Salteena rolling over in the costly bed. Mr Clark is nearly out of the bath sir anounced Horace I will have great plesure in turning it on for you if such is your desire. Well yes you might said Mr Salteena seeing it was the idear and Horace gave a profound bow.

Ethel are you getting up shouted Mr Salteena.

Very nearly replied Ethel faintly from the next room.

I say said Mr Salteena excitedly I have had some tea in bed.

So have I replied Ethel.

Then Mr Salteena got into a mouve dressing goun with yellow tassles and siezing his soap he wandered off to the bath room which was most sumpshous. It had a lovly white shiny bath and sparkling taps and several towels arrayed in readiness by thourghtful Horace. It also had a step for climbing up the bath and other good dodges of a rich nature. Mr Salteena washed himself well and felt very much better. After brekfast Mr Salteena asked Bernard if he could have some privite conversation with him. Well yes replied Bernard if you will come into my study we can have a few words.

Cant I come too muttered Ethel sulkily.

No my dear said Mr Salteena this is privite.

Perhaps later I might have a privite chat with you Miss Monticue said Bernard kindly.

Oh do lets said Ethel.

Then Bernard and Mr S. strolled to the study and sat upon two arm chairs. Fire away said Bernard lighting his pipe. Well I cant exactly do that said Mr Salteena in slow tones it is a searious matter and you can advise me as you are a thorugh gentleman I am sure.

Well yes said Bernard what can I do for you eh Alf?

You can help me perhaps to be more like a gentleman said Mr Salteena getting rarther hot I am quite alright as they say but I would like to be the real thing can it be done he added slapping his knees.

I dont quite know said Bernard it might take a good time.

Might it said Mr S. but I would slave for years if need be. Bernard scratched his head. Why dont you try the Crystal Pallace he asked several peaple Earls and even dukes have privite compartments there.

But I am not an Earl said Mr Salteena in a purplexed tone.

[41]

True replied Bernard but I understand there are sort of students there who want to get into the War Office and notable banks.

Would that be a help asked Mr Salteena egerly.

Well it might said Bernard I can give you a letter to my old pal the Earl of Clincham who lives there he might rub you up and by mixing with him you would probably grow more seemly.

Oh ten thousand thanks said Mr Salteena I will go there as soon as it can be arranged if you would be so kind as to keep an eye on Ethel while I am away.

Oh yes said Bernard I may be running up to town for a few days and she could come too.

You are too kind said Mr Salteena and I dont think you will find her any trouble.

No I dont think I shall said Bernard she is a pretty girl cheerful and active.   And he blushed rarther red.

# CHAPTER 5

## THE CRYSTAL PALACE

ABOUT 9 oclock next morning Mr Salteena stood bag in hand in the ancestle hall waiting for the viacle to convay him to the station. Bernard Clark and Ethel were seated side by side on a costly sofa gazing abstractly at the parting guest. Horace had dashed off to put on his cocked hat as he was going in the baroushe but Francis Minnit was roaming about the hall well prepared for any deed.

Well said Bernard puffing at his meershum pipe I hope you will get on Alf I am sure you have that little letter to old Clincham eh

In deed I have said Mr Salteena many thanks for the same and I do hope Ethel will behave properly.

[43]

Oh yes I expect she will said Bernard with a sigh.

I always do said Ethel in a snappy tone.

Just then there was a great clatter outside and the sound of hoofs and a loud neigh. The barouche I take it said Bernard rising slowly.

Quite correct sir said Minnit flinging wide the portles.

Well goodbye Alf old man said Bernard Clark good luck and God bless you he added in a pius tone.

Not at all said Mr Salteena I have enjoyed my stop which has been short and sweet well goodbye Ethel my child he said as bag in hand he proceeded to the door. Francis Minnit bowed low and handed a small parcel to Mr Salteena a few sandwighs for the jorney sir he remarked.

Oh this is most kind said Mr Salteena.

Minnit closed his eyes with a tired smile. Not kind sir he muttered quite usual.

Oh really said Mr Salteena feeling rather

[44]

flabergasted well goodbye my good fellow and he slipped 2/6 into the butlers open palm.

Mr Salteena had to travel first class as active Horace ran on to buy the ticket which he presented with a low bow the *Times* and *Tit-Bits*. Oh many thanks my man said Mr Salteena in a most airy voice now will you find me a corner seat in the train eh.

If there is one sir replied Horace.

In got Mr Salteena to his first class carrage surrounded by his luggage carefully piled up by kindly Horace. The other pasengers looked full of envy at the curly white wig and green plush uniform of Horace. Mr Salteena crossed his legs in a lordly way and flung a fur rug over his knees though he was hot enough in all consciunce. He began to feel this was the thin end of the partition and he smiled as he gently tapped the letter in his coat tail pocket. When Mr Salteena arrived in

London he began to strolle up the principle streets thinking how gay all was. Presently he beheld a resterant with a big Menu outside and he went boldly in.

It was a sumpshous spot all done up in gold with plenty of looking glasses. Many hansome ladies and gentlemen were already partaking of choice food and rich wines and whiskey and the scene was most lively. Mr Salteena had a little whiskey to make him feel more at home. Then he eat some curry to the tune of a merry valse on the band. He beat time to the music and smiled kindly at the waiters and he felt very excited inside. I am seeing life with a vengance he muttered to himself as he paid his bill at the desk. Outside Mr Salteena found a tall policeman. Could you direct me to the Crystale Pallace if you please said Mr Salteena nervously.

Well said the geniul policeman my advice would be to take a cab sir.

Oh would it said Mr Salteena then I will do so.

He hailed a Hansome and got speedily in to the Crystal Palace he cried gaily and holding his bag on his knees he prepared to enjoy the sights of the Metropilis. It was a merry drive and all too soon the Palace heaved in view. Mr Salteena sprang out and paid the man and then he entered the wondrous edifice. His heart beat very fast as two huge men in gold braid flung open the doors. Inside was a lovely fountain in the middle and all round were little stalls where you could buy sweets and lemonade also scent handkerchiefs and many dainty articles. There were a lot of peaple but nobody very noteable.

At last after buying two bottles of scent and some rarther nice sweets which stuck to his teeth Mr Salteena beheld a wooden door on which was nailed a notice saying To the Privite Compartments.

Ah ha said Mr Salteena to himself this is

evidently my next move, and he gently pushed open the door straitening his top hat as he did so. Inside he found himself in a dimly lit passage with a thick and handsom carpet. Mr Salteena gazed round and beheld in the gloom a very superier gentleman in full evening dress who was reading a newspaper and warming his hands on the hot water pipes. Mr Salteena advanced on tiptoe and coughed gently as so far the gentleman had paid no attention. However at the second cough he raised his eyes in a weary fashion. do you want anything he asked in a most noble voice.

Mr Salteena got very flustered. Well I am seeking the Earl of Clincham he began in a trembly voice are you by any chance him he added most respectfully.

No not exacktly replied the other my name happens to be Edward Procurio. I am half italian and I am the Groom of the Chambers.

What chambers asked Mr Salteena blinking his eyes.

These said Edward Procurio waving a thin arm.

Mr Salteena then noticed several red doors with names of people on each one. Oh I see he said then perhaps you can tell me where the Earl of Clincham is to be found.

At the end of the passage fourth door down said Procurio tritely of course he may be out one never knows what they are up to.

I suppose not said Mr Salteena in an interested tone.

One can not gamble on anything really said Procurio returning to the hot water pipes though of course I know a lot more than most peaple about the inmates here.

What are the habbits of the Earl of Clincham said Mr Salteena.

Procurio gave a smile many and varius he replied I cant say much in my position

[49]

but one lives and learns. He heaved a sigh and shruged his shoulders.

Well good day said Mr Salteena feeling better for the chat.

Procurio nodded in silence as Mr Salteena trotted off down the passage. At last he came to a door labelled Clincham Earl of in big letters. With a beating heart Mr Salteena pulled the bell and the door swung open of its own accord. At the same moment a cheery voice rang out from the distance. Come in please I am in the study first door on left.

With a nervous bound Mr Salteena obeyd these directions and found himself in a small but handsome compartment done in dark green lether with crests on the chairs. Over the mantlepiece was hung the painting of a lady in a low neck looking quite the thing. By the desk was seated a tall man of 35 with very nice eyes of a twinkly nature and curly hair he wore a quite plain suit of palest grey but well

[50]

made and on the table reposed a grey top hat which had evidently been on his head recently. He had a rose in his button hole also a signet ring.

Hullo said this pleasant fellow as Mr. Salteena was spell bound on mat.

Hullo your Lord Ship responded our hero bowing low and dropping his top hat do I adress the Earl of Clincham.

You do said the Earl with a homely smile and who do I adress eh.

Our hero bowed again Alfred Salteena he said in deep tones.

Oh I see said the kindly earl well come in my man and tell me who you are.

Mr Salteena seated himself gingerly on the edge of a crested chair.

To tell you the truth my Lord I am not anyone of import and I am not a gentleman as they say he ended getting very red and hot.

Have some whiskey said lord Clincham and he poured the liquid into a glass at his elbow. Mr. Salteena lapped it up thankfully.

Well my man said the good natured earl what I say is what dose it matter we cant all be of the Blood royal can we.

No said Mr Salteena but I suppose you are.

Lord Clincham waved a careless hand. A small portion flows in my viens he said but it dose not worry me at all and after all he added piously at the Day of Judgement what will be the odds.

Mr Salteena heaved a sigh. I was thinking of this world he said.

Oh I see said the Earl but my own idear is that these things are as piffle before the wind.

Not being an earl I cant say answered our hero but may I beg you to read this letter my Lord. He produced Bernards note from his coat tails. The Earl of Clincham took it in his long fingers. This is what he read.

MY DEAR CLINCHAM

The bearer of this letter is an old friend of mine not quite the right side of the blanket as they say in fact he is the son of a first rate butcher but his mother was a decent family called Hyssopps of the Glen so you see he is not so bad and is desireus of being the correct article. Could you rub him up a bit in Socierty ways. I dont know much details about him but no doubt he will supply all you need. I am keeping well and hope you are. I must run up to the Compartments one day and look you up.

Yours as ever your faithfull friend
BERNARD CLARK.

The Earl gave a slight cough and gazed at Mr Salteena thourghtfully.

Have you much money he asked and are you prepared to spend a good deal.

Oh yes quite gasped Mr Salteena I have plenty in the bank and £10 in ready gold in my purse.

[53]

You see these compartments are the haunts of the Aristockracy said the earl and they are kept going by peaple who have got something funny in their family and who want to be less mere if you can comprehend.

Indeed I can said Mr Salteena.

Personally I am a bit parshial to mere people said his Lordship but the point is that we charge a goodly sum for our training here but however if you cant pay you need not join.

I can and will proclaimed Mr Salteena and he placed a £10 note on the desk. His Lordship slipped it in his trouser pocket. It will be £42 before I have done with you he said but you can pay me here and there as convenient.

Oh thankyou cried Mr Salteena.

Not at all said the Earl and now to bissness. While here you will live in compartments in the basement known as Lower Range. You will get many hints from the Groom of the Chambers as to clothes and ettiquett to menials. You will mix with me for grammer and I might take you out hunting or shooting sometimes to give you a few tips. Also I have lots of ladies partys which you will attend occasionally.

Mr Salteenas eyes flashed with excitement. I shall enjoy that he cried.

His Lordship coughed loudly. You may not marry while under instruction he said firmly.

Oh I shall not need to thankyou said Mr Salteena.

You must also decide on a profeshion said his Lordship as your instruction will vary according.

Could I be anything at Buckingham Pallace said Mr Salteena with flashing eyes.

Oh well I dont quite know said the noble earl but you might perhaps gallopp beside the royal baroushe if you care to try.

Oh indeed I should cried Mr Salteena I am very fond of fresh air and royalties.

Well said the earl with a knowing smile

[55]

I might arrange it with the prince of Wales who I am rarther intimate with.

Not really gasped Mr Salteena.

Dear me yes remarked the earl carelessly and if we decide for you to gallopp by the royal viacle you must be mesured for some plush knickerbockers at once.

Mr Salteena glanced at his rarther fat legs and sighed.

Well I must go out now and call on a few Dowigers said his Lordship picking up his elegent top hat. Well au revoir he added with a good french accent.

Adieu my Lord cried Mr Salteena not to be out done we meet anon I take it.

Not till tomorrow answered the earl you will now proceed to the lower regions where you will no doubt find tea. He nodded kindly and glided out in silence.

Here I will end my chapter.

# CHAPTER 6

Mr Salteena awoke next morning in his
small but pleasant room. It was done in
green and white with Monagrams on the
toilit set. He had a tiny white bed with a
green quilt and a picture of the Nativaty
and one of Windsor Castle on the walls.
The sun was shining over all these things
as Mr Salteena opened his sleepy eyes. Just
then there was rat tat on the door. Come
in called Mr Salteena and in came Edward
Procurio ballancing a tray very cleverly.
He looked most elegant with his shiny black
hair and pale yellow face and half shut
eyes. He smiled in a very mysterious and
superier way as he placed the tray on Mr
Salteenas pointed knees.

Your early beverage he announced and

[57]

began to pull up the blinds still smiling to himself.

Oh thankyou cried Mr Salteena feeling very towzld compared to this grand fellow. Then to his great supprise Procurio began to open the wardrobe and look at Mr Salteenas suits making italian exclamations under his breath. Mr Salteena dare not say a word so he swollowed his tea and eat a Marie biscuit hastilly. Presently Procurio advanced to the bed with a bright blue serge suit. Will you wear this today sir he asked quietly.

Oh certainly said Mr Salteena.

And a clean shirt would not come amiss said Procurio what about this pale blue and white stripe.

With pleashure replied Mr Salteena. So Procurio laid them out in neat array also a razer and brush for shaving. Then he opened a door saying This is the bath room shall I turn on hot or cold.

[58]

I dont mind said Mr Salteena feeling very hot and ignorant.

It is best for you to decide sir said Procurio firmly.

Well I will try cold said Mr Salteena feeling it was more manly to say that. Procurio bowed and beat a retreat to the bath room. Then he returned and told Mr. Salteena that when he was washed he would find his breakfast in the sitting room. When Mr Salteena was dressed in his best blue suit and clean shirt he stroled into the sitting room where a gay canary was singing fit to burst in the window and a copple of doves cooing in a whicker cage. A cheery smell greeted him as Procurio glided in with some steaming coffie. Mr Salteena felt more at home and passed a few remarks about the weather. Procurio smiled and uncovered some lovely kidnys on toast and as he did so bent and whispered in Mr Salteenas ear you could have come in in your dressing gown.

Mr Salteena gave a start. Oh can I he said ten thousand thanks.

Then Procurio passed out and Mr Salteena finnished his kidneys and chiruped to the birds and had a cigarette from a handsome purple box which he found on the desk. Then Procurio entered once more and with a bow said. His lordship is going to a levie this morning and thinks it might amuse you to go too. Could you be ready by 11 oclock.

Oh yes what fun said Mr Salteena have you any notion what a levie is my man.

Procurio gave a superier smile. It is a party given by the Queen to very superier peaple but this one is given by the Prince of Wales as the Queen is not quite her usual self today. It will be at Buckingham palace so you will drive with his lordship.

Mr Salteena was fearfully excited. What shall I weare he gasped.

Well of course you ought to have black satin knickerbockers and a hat with white feathers also garters and a star or two.

You supprise me said Mr Salteena I have none of those articles.

Well said Procurio kindly his lordship will lend you his second best cocked hat as you are obliged to wear one and I think with a little thourght I might rig you up so as to pass muster.

Then they rumaged among Mr Salteenas things and Procurio got very intelligent and advised Mr Salteena to were his black evening suit and role up his trousers. He also lent him a pair of white silk stockings which he fastened tightly round his knees with red rosettes. Then he quickly cut out a star in silver paper and pinned it to his chest and also added a strip of red ribbon across his shirt front. Then Mr Salteena survayed himself in the glass. Is it a fancy dress party he asked.

No they always were that kind of thing but wait till you see his Lordship—if you are ready sir I will conduct you in.

Mr Salteena followed Procurio up countless stairs till they came to the Earls compartments and tapped on the bedroom door.

Come in cried a merry voice and in they
strode.

I have done my best with Mr Salteena
my lord I trust he will do the hat of course
will make a deal of diffrence.

Mr Salteena bowed nervously wishing he
had got correct knickerbockers as his trousers did not feel too firm in spite of the garters.

Not half bad cried the earl try on the
hat Salteena it is on my bed. Mr Salteena
placed it on his head and the feathers and
gold braid became him very well but he
felt very jellous of the earl who looked a
sight for the gods. He had proper satin
knickerbockers with diamond clasps and
buckled shoes and black silk stockings
which showed up his long fine legs. He had
a floppy shirt of softist muslin with real
lace collar and cuffs. A sword hung at

his side and a crimson sash was round his
waist and a splendid cocked hat on his head.
His blue eyes twinkled as he pulled on a
pair of white kid gloves.

Well come on Salteena he cried and dont
be nervus I will get you a pair of knickers
tomorrow. Will you get a hansome Procurio.

Presently the earl and Mr Salteena were
clattering away to Buckingham palace.

You wont mind if I introduce you as
Lord Hyssops do you said the earl as he
lit his pipe. You see you are sort of mixed
up with the family so it wont matter and
will look better.

So it would said Mr Salteena what do we
do at the levie.

Oh we strole round and eat ices and
champaigne and that kind of thing and
sometimes there is a little music.

Is there any dancing asked Mr Salteena.

Well not always said the Earl.

I am glad of that said Mr Salteena I am

not so nimble as I was and my garters are a trifle tight.

Sometimes we talk about the laws and politics said the earl if Her Majesty is in that kind of a mood.

Just then the splendid edifice appeared in view and Mr Salteena licked his dry lips at sight of the vast crowd. All round were carrages full of costly peaple and outside the railings stood tall Life Guards keeping off the mere peaple who had gathered to watch the nobility clatter up. Lord Clincham began to bow right and left raising his cocked hat to his friends. There was a lot of laughter and friendly words as the cab finally drew up at the front door. Two tall life guards whisked open the doors and one of them kindly tipped the cabman. Mr Salteena followed his lordship up the grand steps trying to feel as homely as he could. Then a splendid looking fellow in a red tunick and a sort of black velvit tam a shanter stepped forward from the throng shouting what name please.

The Earl of Clincham and Lord Hyssops calmly replied the earl gently nudging Mr Salteena to act up. Mr Salteena nodded and blinked at the menial as much as to say all is well and then he and the earl hung up their cocked hats on two pegs. This way cried a deep voice and another menial apeared wearing stiff white britches top boots and a green velvit coat with a leather belt also a very shiny top hat. They followed this fellow down countless corridoors and finally came to big folding doors. The earl twiddled his mustache and slapped his leg with his white glove as calmly as could be. Mr Salteena purspired rarther hard and gave a hitch to his garters to make sure.

Then the portles divided and their names were shouted in chorus by countless domesticks. The sumshious room was packed with men of a noble nature dressed like the earl in satin knickerboccers etc and with

ladies of every hue with long trains and
jewels by the dozen. You could hardly
moove in the gay throng. Dukes were as
nought as there were a good lot of princes
and Arch Dukes as it was a very superier
levie indeed. The earl and Mr Salteena
struggled through the crowd till they came
to a platform draped with white velvit.
Here on a golden chair was seated the
prince of Wales in a lovely ermine cloak
and a small but costly crown. He was chat-
ting quite genially with some of the crowd.

Up clambered the earl followed at top
speed by Mr Salteena.

Hullo Clincham cried the Prince quite
homely and not at all grand so glad you
turned up—quite a squash eh.

A bit over powering your Highness said
the earl who was quite used to all this may
I introduce my friend Lord Hyssops he is
staying with me so I thought I would bring
him along if you dont mind Prince.

Not at all cried the genial prince looking

rarther supprised. Mr Salteena bowed so low he nearly fell off the platform and as the prince put out a hand Mr Salteena thought he had better kiss it. The Prince smiled kindly I am pleased to see you Lord Hyssops he said in a regal voice.

Then the Earl chipped in and how is the dear Queen he said reveruntly.

Not up to much said his Highness she feels the heat poor soul and he waved to a placard which said in large letters The Queen is indisposed.

Presently his Highness rose I think I will have a quiet glass of champaigne he said you come too Clincham and bring your friend the Diplomats are arriving and I am not much in the mood for deep talk I have already signed a dozen documents so I have done my duty.

They all went out by a private door and found themselves in a smaller but gorgous room. The Prince tapped on the table and instantly two menials in red tunics appeared. Bring three glasses of champaigne commanded the prince and some ices he added majestikally. The goods appeared as if by majic and the prince drew out a cigar case and passed it round.

One grows weary of Court Life he remarked.

Ah yes agreed the earl.

It upsets me said the prince lapping up his strawberry ice all I want is peace and quiut and a little fun and here I am tied down to this life he said taking off his crown being royal has many painfull drawbacks.

True mused the Earl.

Silence fell and the strains of the band could be heard from the next room. Suddenly the prince gazed at Mr Salteena. Who did you say you were he asked in a puzzled tone.

Lord Hyssops responded our hero growing purple at the lie.

Well you are not a bit like the Lord

Hyssops I know replied the Prince could you explain matters.

Mr Salteena gazed helplessly at the earl who had grown very pale and seemed lost for the moment. However he quickly recovered.

He is quite alright really Prince he said His mother was called Miss Hyssops of the Glen.

Indeed said his royal Highness that sounds correct but who was your father eh.

Then Mr Salteena thourght he would not tell a lie so in trembly tones he muttered My poor father was but a butcher your Highness a very honest one I may add and passing rich he was called Domonic Salteena and my name is Alfred Salteena.

The Prince stroked his yellow beard and rarther admired Mr Salteena for his truthful utterance—Oh I see he said well why did you palm off on my menials as Lord Hyssops eh

Mr Salteena wiped his swetting brow but

the earl came to the rescue nobly. My fault entirely Prince he chimed in, as I was bringing him to this very supearier levie I thought it would be better to say he was of noble birth have I offended your Royal dignity.

Not much said the prince it was a laudible notion and perhaps I will ask Mr Salteena to one of my big balls some day.

Oh your Highness gasped our hero falling on one knee that would indeed be a treat.

I suppose Prince you have not got a job going at this palace for my friend asked the earl you see I am rubbing him up in socierty ways and he fancies court life as a professhon.

Oh dose he said the prince blinking his eyes well I might see.

I suggested if there was a vacency going he might try cantering after the royal barouche said the earl.

So he might said the prince I will speak

[70]

to the prime Minister about it and let you know.

Ten thousand thanks cried Mr Salteena bowing low.

Well now I must get along back to the levie announced the prince putting on his crown I have booked a valse with the Arch duchess of Greenwich and this is her favorite tune. So saying they issued back to the big room where the nobility were whirling gaily roand the more searious peaple such as the prime minister and the admirals etc were eating ices and talking passionately about the laws in a low undertone.

The earl was soon mingling gaily in a set of lancers but Mr Salteena dare not because of his trousers. However he sat on a velvit chair and quite enjoyed over hearing the intelligent conversation of the prime minister. And now we will leave our hero enjoying his glimpse of high life and return to Ethel Monticue.

## CHAPTER 7

AFTER Mr Salteena had departed Bernard
Clark thourght he would show Ethel over
his house so they spent a merry morning so
doing. Ethel passed bright remarks on all
the rooms and Bernard thourght she was
most pretty and Ethel began to be a bit
excited. After a lovly lunch they sat in the
gloomy hall and Ethel began to feel very
glad Mr Salteena was not there. Suddenly
Bernard lit his pipe I was thinking he said
passionately what about going up to London for a weeks Gaierty.

Who inquired Ethel in a low tone.

You and me said Bernard I know of several splendid hotels and we could go to
theaters and parties and enjoy ourselves to
the full.

So we could what an idear cried Ethel.

So the merry plan was all arranged and they spent the afternoon in packing there trunks. Next day they were all ready in the hall when the handsome viacle once more clattered up. Ethel had on her blue velvit get up and a sweet new hat and plenty of ruge on her face and looked quite a seemly counterpart for Bernard who was arrayed in a white and shiny mackintosh top boots and a well brushed top hat tied on to him with a bit of black elastick.

Well goodbye Minnit he cried to the somber butler take care of your gout and the silver and I will pay your wages when I come back.

Thankyou kindly sir murmured Minnit when may I expect your return.

Oh well I will wire he said and dashed doun the steps.

Ethel followed with small lady like steps having bowed perlitely to Minnit who closed his eyes in acknowlegment of her kindness.

[73]

The sun was shining and Ethel had the feeling of going to a very jolly party and felt so sorry for all the passers by who were not going to London with Bernard.

Arrived in the gay city Bernard hailed a cab to the manner born and got in followed by Ethel. Kindly drive us to the Gaierty Hotel he cried in a firm tone. The cabman waved his whip and off they dashed.

We shall be highly comfortable and select at the Gaierty said Bernard and he thourght to himself how lovly it would be if he was married to Ethel. He blushed a deep shade at his own thourghts and gave a side long glance at Ethel who was gazing out of the window. Well one never knows he murmerd to himself and as one of the poets says great events from trivil causes springs.

Just then they stopped at the gay hotel and Ethel was spellbound at the size of the big hall—Bernard poked his head into the window of the pay desk. Have you a coup-

ple of bedrooms for self and young lady he
enquired in a lordly way.

A very handsome lady with golden hair
and a lace apron glanced at a book and
hastilly replied Oh yes sir two beauties on
the 1st floor number 9 and 10.

Thankyou said Bernard we will go up if
you have no objection.

None whatever sir said the genial lady
the beds are well aired and the view is quite
pleasant.

Come along Ethel cried Bernard this
sounds alright eh.

Oh quite said Ethel with a beaming smile.

They went upstairs and entered number
9 a very fine compartment with a large
douny bed and white doors with glass han-
dles leading into number 10 an equally
dainty room but a trifle smaller.

Which will you have Ethel asked Bernard.

Oh well I would rarther you settled it

said Ethel. I am willing to abide by your choice.

The best shall be yours then said Bernard bowing gallantly and pointing to the biggest room.

Ethel blushed at his speaking look. I shall be quite lost in that huge bed she added to hide her embarassment.

Yes I expect you will said Bernard and now what about a little table d'ote followed by a theater.

Oh yes cried Ethel and downstairs they went.

# CHAPTER 8

## A GAY CALL

I TELL you what Ethel said Bernard Clark about a week later we might go and pay a call on my pal the Earl of Clincham.

Oh do lets cried Ethel who was game for any new adventure I would dearly love to meet his lordship.

Bernard gave a frown of jellousy at her rarther mere words.

Well dress in your best he muttered.

Ethel skipped into her bedroom and arrayd herself in a grass green muslin of decent cut a lace scarf long faun colored kid gloves and a muslin hat to correspond. She carried a parasole in one hand also a green silk bag containing a few stray hair pins a clean handkerchief five shillings and a pot of ruge in case. She looked a dainty vishen

with her fair hair waving in the breeze
and Bernard bit his lips rarther hard for
he could hardly contain himself and felt he
must marry Ethel soon. He looked a handsome sight himself in some exquisite white
trousers with a silk shirt and a pale blue
blazer belt and cap. He wore this in honour
of the earl who had been to Cambridge in
his youth and so had Bernard Clark.

At last they found themselves in the en-
trance hall of the Crystale palace and
speedily made their way to the privite compartments. Edward Procurio was walking
up and down the passage looking dark and
mystearious as usual.

Is His Lordship at home cried Bernard
Clark cheerily.

Which one asked Procurio many lords
live here he said scornfully.

Well I mean the Earl of Clincham said
Bernard.

Oh yes he is in responded Procurio and
to the best of my belief giving a party.

[78]

Indeed ejaculated Bernard we have come in the nick of time Ethel he added. Yes said Ethel in an excited tone.

Then they pealed on the bell and the door flew open. Sounds of laughter and comic songs issued from the abode and in a second they were in the crowded drawing room. It was packed with all the Elite and a stout duchess with a good natured face was singing a lively song and causing much merriment. The earl strode forward at sight of two new comers. Hullo Bernard old boy he cried this is a pleasure and who have you got with you he added glancing at Ethel.

Oh this is Miss Monticue said Bernard shall I introduce you——

If you will be so good said the Earl in an affable tone and Bernard hastily performed the right. Ethel began a bright conversatiun while Bernard stroled off to see if he could find any friends amid the throng.

[79]

What pleasant compartments you have cried Ethel in rarther a socierty tone.

Fairly so so responded the Earl do you live in London he added in a loud tone as someone was playing a very difficult peice on the piano.

Well no I dont said Ethel my home is really in Northumberland but I am at present stopping with Mr Clark at the Gaierty Hotel she continud in a somewhat showing off tone.

Oh I see said the earl well shall I introduce you to a few of my friends.

Of please do said Ethel with a dainty blow at her nose.

The earl disserppeard into the madding crowd and presently came back with a middle aged gentleman. This is Lord Hyssops he said my friend Miss Monticue he added genially.

Ethel turned a dull yellaw. Lord Hyssops she said in a faint voice why it is Mr Salteena I know him well.

[80]

Hush cried the Earl it is a title bestowd recently by my friend the Prince of Wales.

Yes indeed murmered Mr Salteena deeply flabbergasted by the ready wit of the earl.

Oh indeed said Ethel in a peevish tone well how do you come to be here.

I am stopping with his Lordship said Mr Salteena and have a set of compartments in the basement so there.

I dont care said huffy Ethel I am in handsome rooms at the Gaierty.

Nothing could be nicer I am sure struck in the earl what do you say Hyssops eh.

Doubtless it is charming said Mr Salteena who was wanting peace tell me Ethel how did you leave Bernard.

I have not left him said Ethel in an annoying voice I am stopping with him at the gaierty and we have been to lots of theaters and dances.

Well I am glad you are enjoying yourself said Mr Salteena kindly you had been looking pale of late.

No wonder in your stuffy domain cried
Ethel well have you got any more friends
she added turning to the earl.

Well I will see said the obliging earl and
he once more disapeared.

I dont know why you should turn against
me Ethel said Mr Salteena in a low tone.

Ethel patted her hair and looked very
sneery. Well I call it very mystearious
you going off and getting a title said Ethel
and I think our friendship had better stop
as no doubt you will soon be marrying a
duchess or something.

Not at all said Mr Salteena you must
know Ethel he said blushing a deep red I
always wished to marry you some fine day.

This is news to me cried Ethel still peevish.

But not to me murmered Mr Salteena
and his voice trembled in his chest. I may
add that I have always loved you and now
I seem to do so madly he added passionately.

[82]

But I dont love you responded Ethel.

But if you married me you might get to said Mr Salteena.

I think not replied Ethel and all the same it is very kind of you to ask me and she smiled more nicely at him.

This is agony cried Mr Salteena clutching hold of a table my life will be sour grapes and ashes without you.

Be a man said Ethel in a gentle whisper and I shall always think of you in a warm manner.

Well half a loaf is better than no bread responded Mr Salteena in a gloomy voice and just then the earl reappeard with a very brisk lady in a tight silk dress whose name was called Lady Gay Finchling and her husband was a General but had been dead a few years. So this is Miss Monticue she began in a rarther high voice. Oh yes said Ethel and Mr Salteena wiped the foaming dew from his forehead. Little did Lady

[83]

Gay Finchling guess she had just disturbed a proposal of marrage.

The Earl chimed into the conversation now and again and Lady Gay Finchling told several rarther witty stories to enliven the party. Then Bernard Clark came up and said they had better be going.

Well goodbye Clincham he said I must say I have enjoyed this party most rechauffie I call it dont you Ethel.

Most cried Ethel I suppose you often come she added in a tone of envy to Lady Gay Finchling.

Pretty often said Lady G. F. well goodbye as I see you are in a hurry to be off and she dashed off towards the refreshment place.

Goodbye Ethel said poor Mr Salteena in a spasam and he seized hold of her hand you will one day rue your wicked words farewell he repeated emphatically.

Oh well goodbye said Ethel in a vage tone and then turning to the earl she said

[84]

I have enjoyed myself very much thankyou.

Please dont mention it cried the earl well goodbye Bernard he added I shall look you up some day at your hotel.

Yes do muttered Bernard always welcome Clincham old boy he added placing his blue crickit cap on his head and so saying he and Ethel left the gay scene and once more oozed fourth into the streets of London.

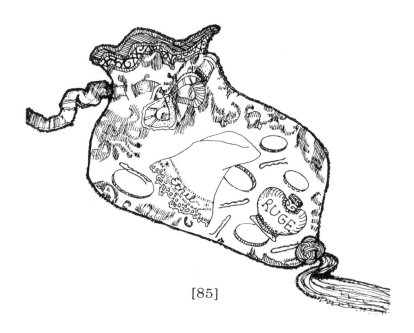

## CHAPTER 9

### A PROPOSALE

NEXT morning while imbibing his morning
tea beneath his pink silken quilt Bernard
decided he must marry Ethel with no more
delay.  I love the girl he said to himself
and she must be mine but I somehow feel I
can not propose in London it would not be
seemly in the city of London.  We must go
for a day in the country and when surrounded by the gay twittering of the birds and
the smell of the cows I will lay my suit at
her feet and he waved his arm wildly at the
gay thought.  Then he sprang from bed and
gave a rat tat at Ethels door.

Are you up my dear he called.

Well not quite said Ethel hastilly jump-
ing from her downy nest.

Be quick cried Bernard I have a plan to

spend a day near Windsor Castle and we
will take our lunch and spend a happy day.

Oh Hurrah shouted Ethel I shall soon be
ready as I had my bath last night so wont
wash very much now.

No dont said Bernard and added in a
rarther fervent tone through the chink of
the door you are fresher than the rose my
dear no soap could make you fairer.

Then he dashed off very embarrased to
dress. Ethel blushed and felt a bit excited
as she heard the words and she put on a
new white muslin dress in a fit of high
spirits. She looked very beautifull with
some red roses in her hat and the dainty
red ruge in her cheeks looked quite the
thing. Bernard heaved a sigh and his eyes
flashed as he beheld her and Ethel thorght
to herself what a fine type of manhood he
reprisented with his nice thin legs in pale
broun trousers and well fitting spats and a
red rose in his button hole and rarther a
sporting cap which gave him a great air

[87]

with its quaint check and little flaps to pull down if necesarry. Off they started the envy of all the waiters.

They arrived at Windsor very hot from the jorney and Bernard at once hired a boat to row his beloved up the river. Ethel could not row but she much enjoyed seeing the tough sunburnt arms of Bernard tugging at the oars as she lay among the rich cushons of the dainty boat. She had a rarther lazy nature but Bernard did not know of this. However he soon got dog tired and sugested lunch by the mossy bank.

Oh yes said Ethel quickly opening the sparkling champaigne.

Dont spill any cried Bernard as he carved some chicken.

They eat and drank deeply of the charming viands ending up with merangs and choclates.

Let us now bask under the spreading trees said Bernard in a passiunate tone.

Oh yes lets said Ethel and she opened her

[88]

dainty parasole and sank down upon the long green grass. She closed her eyes but she was far from asleep. Bernard sat beside her in profound silence gazing at her pink face and long wavy eye lashes. He puffed at his pipe for some moments while the larks gaily caroled in the blue sky. Then he edged a trifle closer to Ethels form.

Ethel he murmured in a trembly voice.

Oh what is it said Ethel hastily sitting up.

Words fail me ejaculated Bernard horsly my passion for you is intense he added fervently. It has grown day and night since I first beheld you.

Oh said Ethel in supprise I am not prepared for this and she lent back against the trunk of the tree.

Bernard placed one arm tightly round her. When will you marry me Ethel he uttered you must be my wife it has come to that I love you so intensly that if you say no I shall perforce dash my body to the brink of yon muddy river he panted wildly.

Oh dont do that implored Ethel breathing rarther hard.

Then say you love me he cried.

Oh Bernard she sighed fervently I certinly love you madly you are to me like a Heathen god she cried looking at his manly form and handsome flashing face I will indeed marry you.

How soon gasped Bernard gazing at her intensly.

As soon as possible said Ethel gently closing her eyes.

My Darling whispered Bernard and he seiezed her in his arms we will be marrid next week.

Oh Bernard muttered Ethel this is so sudden.

No no cried Bernard and taking the bull by both horns he kissed her violently on her dainty face. My bride to be he murmered several times.

[90]

Ethel trembled with joy as she heard the mistick words.

Oh Bernard she said little did I ever dream of such as this and she suddenly fainted into his out stretched arms.

Oh I say gasped Bernard and laying the dainty burden on the grass he dashed to the waters edge and got a cup full of the fragrant river to pour on his true loves pallid brow.

She soon came to and looked up with a sickly smile Take me back to the Gaierty hotel she whispered faintly.

With plesure my darling said Bernard I will just pack up our viands ere I unloose the boat.

Ethel felt better after a few drops of champagne and began to tidy her hair while Bernard packed the remains of the food. Then arm in arm they tottered to the boat.

I trust you have not got an illness my darling murmured Bernard as he helped her in.

Oh no I am very strong said Ethel I fainted from joy she added to explain matters.

Oh I see said Bernard handing her a cushon well some people do he added kindly and so saying they rowed down the dark stream now flowing silently beneath a golden moon. All was silent as the lovers glided home with joy in their hearts and radiunce on their faces only the sound of the mystearious water lapping against the frail vessel broke the monotony of the night.

So I will end my chapter.

# CHAPTER 10

THE next few days were indeed bussy for
Ethel and Bernard. First of all Ethel got
some dainty pink note paper with silver
crest on it and sent out invitations in the
following terms to all their frends.

> Miss Ethel Monticue will be married to
> Mr Bernard Clark at Westminster Abbey
> on June 10th. Your company is request-
> ed there at 2-30 sharp and afterwards
> for refreshment at the Gaierty Hotel.
> R.S.V.P.

Having posted heaps of these and got several replies Ethel began to order her wedding dress which cost a good bit. She chose
a rich satin with a humped pattern of gold
on the pure white and it had a long train

[93]

edged with Airum lilies. Her veil was of
pure lace with a crown of orange blossum.
Her bouquett she ordered to be of white
dog daisies St. Joseph lilies and orange
blossums tied up with pale blue satin ribbon.

You will indeed be a charming spectacle
my darling gasped Bernard as they left the
shop. Then they drove to the tailor where
Bernard ordered an elligant black suit with
coat tails lined with crimson satin and a
pale lavender tie and an opera hat of the
same hue and he intended to wear violets in
his buttonholes also his best white spats
diamond studs and a few extras of costly
air. They both ordered a lot of new clothes
besides and Bernard gave Ethel a very huge
tara made of rubies and diamonds also two
rich bracelets and Ethel gave him a bran
new trunk of shiny green leather. The earl
of Clincham sent a charming gift of some
hem stitched sheets edged with real lace and
a photo of himself in a striking attitude.

[94]

Mr Salteena sent Ethel a bible with a few
pious words of advice and regret and he
sent Bernard a very handy little camp stool.
Ethels parents were too poor to come so
far but her Mother sent her a gold watch
which did not go but had been some years
in the family and her father provided a
cheque for £2 and promised to send her a
darling little baby calf when ready. Then
they ordered the most splendid refreshments they had tea and coffie and sparkling
wines to drink also a lovly wedding cake of
great height with a sugar angel at the top
holding a sword made of almond paste.
They had countless cakes besides also ices
jelly merangs jam tarts with plenty of jam
on each some cold tongue some ham with
salid and a pig's head done up in a wondrous manner. Ethel could hardly contain
herself as she gazed at the sumpshious repast and Bernard gave her a glass of rich
wine while he imbibed some whiskey before
going to bed. Ethel got speedilly into her

bed for the last time at the dear old Gaierty
and shed a few salt tears thinking of her
past life but she quickly cheerd up and began to plan about how many children she
would have. I hope I shall have a good lot
she thourght to herself and so saying fell
into repose.

# CHAPTER 11

## THE WEDDING

THE Abbey was indeed thronged next day
when Ethel and Bernard cantered up in a
very fine carriage drawn by two prancing
steeds who foamed a good deal. In the
porch stood several clean altar boys who
conducted the lucky pair up the aile while
the organ pealed a merry blast. The mighty
edifice was packed and seated in the front
row was the Earl of Clincham looking very
brisk as he was going to give Ethel away at
the correct moment. Beside him sat Mr
Salteena all in black and looking bitterly
sad and he ground his teeth as Ethel came
marching up. There were some merry
hymns and as soon as Ethel and Bernard
were one the clergyman began a sermon
about Adam and Eve and the serpent and

Mr Salteena cried into his large handkerchief and the earl kept on nudging him as
his sniffs were rarther loud. Then the wedding march pealed fourth and doun the
church stepped Ethel and Bernard as husband and wife. Into the cab they got and
speedelly dashed off to the Gaierty. The
wedding refreshments were indeed a treat
to all and even Mr Salteena cheered up
when he beheld the wedding cake and sparkling wines. Then the earl got up and made
a very fine speech about marrage vows and
bliss and he quoted several good bits from
the bible which got a lot of applause. Bernard replied in good round terms. I thank
your lordship for those kind remarks he said
in clear tones I expect we shall be as happy
as a lark and I hope you will all be ditto
some day. Here Here muttered a stray lady
in the crowd and down sat Bernard while
Ethel went up to change her wedding gar-
ment for a choice pink velvit dress with a
golden gurdle and a very chick tocque. Ber-

nard also put on a new suit of blue stripe
and some silk socks and clean under cloth-
ing. Hurah hurah shouted the guests as
the pair reappeard in the aforesaid get ups.
Then everybody got a bag of rice and
sprinkled on the pair and Mr Salteena sadly
threw a white tennis shoe at them wiping
his eyes the while. Off drove the happy pair
and the guests finished up the food. The
happy pair went to Egypt for there Honymoon as they thought it would be a nice
warm spot and they had never seen the
wondrous land. Ethel was a bit sick on the
boat but Bernard braved the storm in manly style. However Ethel had recovered by
the time they got to Egypt and here we
will leave them for a merry six weeks of
bliss while we return to England.

## CHAPTER 12

### HOW IT ENDED

Mʀ Sᴀʟᴛᴇᴇɴᴀ by the aid of the earl and the kindness of the Prince of Wales managed to get the job his soul craved and any day might be seen in Hyde park or Pickadilly galloping madly after the Royal Carrage in a smart suit of green velvit with knicker-bockers compleat. At first he was rarther terrified as he was not used to riding and he found his horse bumped him a good deal and he had to cling on desperatly to its flowing main. At other times the horse would stop dead and Mr Salteena would use his spurs and bad languige with no avail. But he soon got more used to his fresh and sultry steed and His Royal Highness seemed satisfide.

The Earl continued his merry life at the

Compartments till finally he fell in love with one of the noble ladies who haunted them. She was not so pretty as Ethel as she had rarther a bulgy figure and brown eyes but she had lovely raven tresses a pointed nose and a rose like complexion of a dainty hue. She had very nice feet and plenty of money. Her name was called Lady Helena Herring and her age was 25 and she mated well with the earl.

Mr Salteena grew very lonely after the earl was marrid and he could not bear a single life any more so failing Ethel he marrid one of the maids in waiting at Buckingham palace by name Bessie Topp a plesant girl of 18 with a round red face and rarther stary eyes.

So now that all our friends are marrid I will add a few words about their familys. Ethel and Bernard returned from their Honymoon with a son and hair a nice fat baby called Ignatius Bernard. They soon had six more children four boys and three girls and some of them were twins which was very exciting.

The Earl only got two rarther sickly girls called Helen and Marie because the last one looked slightly french.

Mr Salteena had a large family of 10 five of each but he grew very morose as the years rolled by and his little cottage was very noisy and his wife was a bit annoying at times especially when he took to dreaming of Ethel and wishing he could have marrid her. Still he was a pius man in his way and found relief in prayer.

Bernard Clark was the happiest of our friends as he loved Ethel to the bitter end and so did she him and they had a nice house too.

The Earl soon got tired of his sickly daughters and his wife had a savage temper so he thourght he would divorce her and try again but he gave up the idear after

[102]

several attempts and decided to offer it up as a Mortification.

So now my readers we will say farewell to the characters in this book.

The End

by Daisy Ashford